For Holly M. McGhee, Caitlyn M. Dlouhy and Emma Hughes
—S. T.

Atheneum Books for Young Readers
An imprint of Simon & Schuster Children's Publishing Division
1230 Avenue of the Americas
New York, New York 10020

Copyright © 2001 by Sandy Turner

The text of this book is set in Times New Roman PS.

Printed in Hong Kong

2 4 6 8 10 9 7 5 3 1

Library of Congress Cataloging-in-Publication Data
Turner, Sandy.
Silent night / by Sandy Turner.—1st ed.
p.   cm.
Summary: Santa tries to deliver presents on Christmas Eve, but he is hindered by a very vocal dog who will not stop barking,
woofing, and yapping.
ISBN 0-689-84156-6
[1. Dogs—Fiction. 2. Santa Claus—Fiction. 3. Christmas—Fiction. 4. Stories without words. 5. Cartoons and comics.] I. Title.
PZ7.T8577 Si 2001
[E]—dc21   2001022479

FIRST
EDITION

SILENT NIGHT

SANDY TURNER

ATHENEUM BOOKS FOR YOUNG READERS
NEW YORK   LONDON   TORONTO   SYDNEY   SINGAPORE

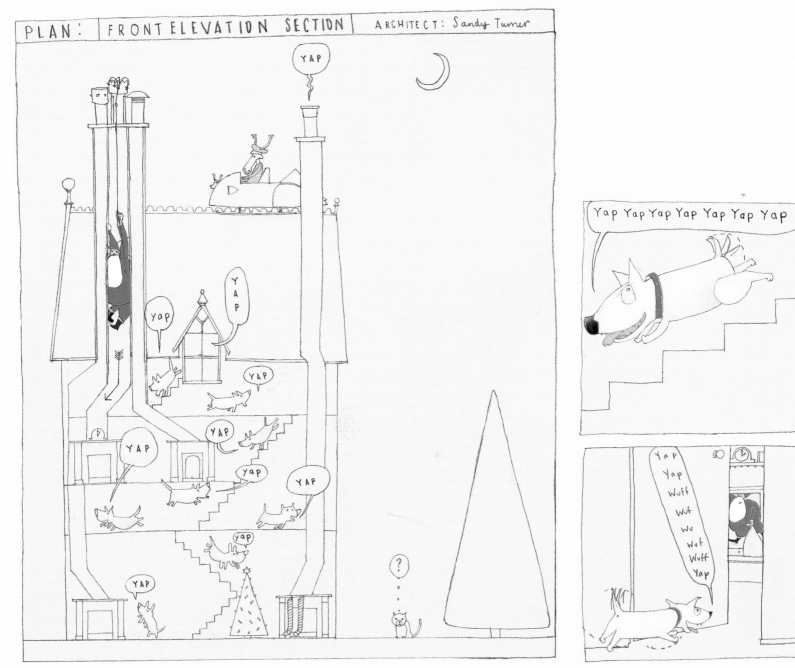

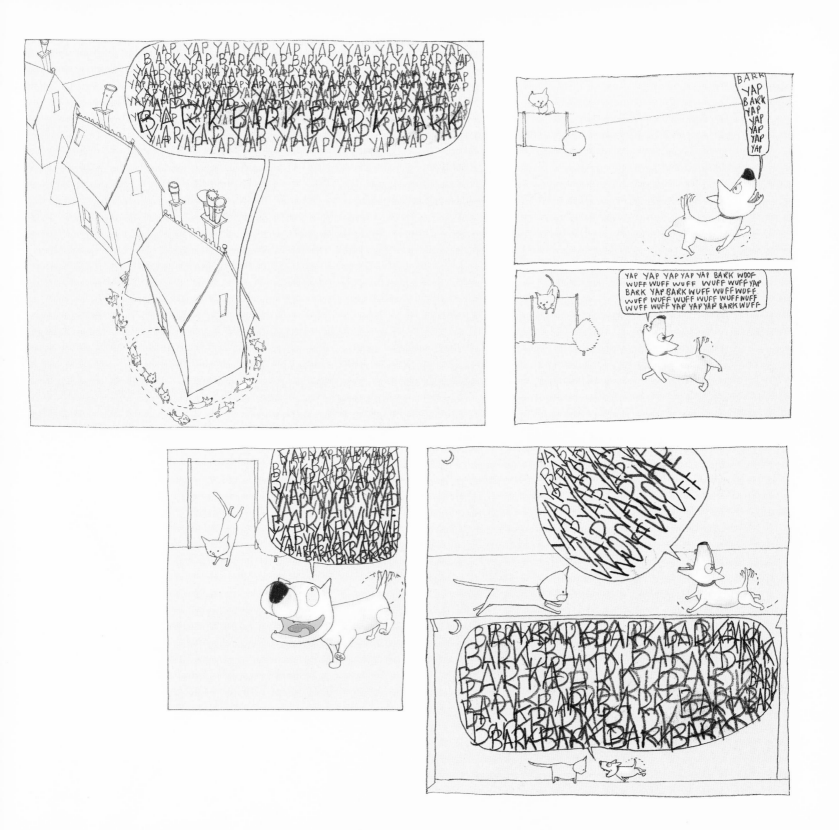